Edgar Lee Masters'

Spoon River

Anthology

Conceived, adapted and arranged

by Charles Aidman

SAMUEL FRENCH, INC.

45 WEST 25TH STREET   NEW YORK 10010

7623 SUNSET BOULEVARD HOLLYWOOD 90046

LONDON   TORONTO

SPOON RIVER ANTHOLOGY was produced for the Broadway stage by Joseph Cates and The Spoon River Anthology Company, and presented at the Booth Theatre, N. Y. C., September 29, 1963.

JOSEPH CATES
presents

BETTY GARRETT	ROBERT ELSTON
JOYCE VAN PATTEN	CHARLES AIDMAN

in
EDGAR LEE MASTERS'

"SPOON RIVER ANTHOLOGY"
with

NAOMI CARYL HIRSHHORN and HAL LYNCH

Conceived and Directed by
CHARLES AIDMAN

Lighting by
JULES FISHER

Original Songs:

Music by
NAOMI CARYL HIRSHHORN

Lyrics by
CHARLES AIDMAN

A CATES BROTHERS PRODUCTION
Originally produced by

THE THEATRE GROUP, UNIVERSITY
EXTENSION, UCLA

Original Cast Album by
COLUMBIA RECORDS

Production Supervised by
ROBERT WEINER

3

RUNNING ORDER

ACT ONE

ENOCH DUNLAP
MRS. KESSLER
NANCY KNAPP
GEORGE CRAY
HARRY WILMANS
NELLIE CLARK
PAPER OF PINS—*Song*
ROSCOE PURCAPILE
MRS. PURCAPILE
A. D. BLOOD
SHACK DYE
FREEDOM
HANNA ARMSTRONG
FAITH MATHENY

RUNNING ORDER
ACT TWO

3 NIGHTS DRUNK—*Song*
JUDGE LIVELY
ZILPHA MARSH
SEARCY FOOTE
MRS. CHARLES BLISS
FAR AWAY FROM HOME—*Song*
PAULINE BARRETT
VILLAGE ATHEIST
MABEL OSBORNE
FRANKLIN JONES
SCHOFIELD HUXLEY
IN THE NIGHT—*Song*
DIPPOLD THE OPTICIAN
IN THE NIGHT—*Song*
ELIJAH BROWNING
GOIN' HOME
ALEXANDER THROCKMORTON
AMANDA BARKER
WILLARD FLUKE
— LOIS SPEARS 44
I SEE THE MOON—*Song*
SOW TOOK THE MEASLES—*Song*

SPOON RIVER SONG ALBUM
Adapted and Arranged by
CHARLES AIDMAN
and
NAOMI CARYL HIRSHHORN
Words and Music Chord Symbols and Guitar
Frames included.

Price $12.95 plus postage

6

Spoon River Anthology

ACT ONE

HE'S GONE AWAY—SONG

TAPED: (*to be sung by* GIRL SINGER).

> He's gone away
> For to stay a little while,
> But he's coming back
> If he goes 10,000 miles.
> But who will buy my shoes,
> And who will glove my hand,
> And who will
> Kiss my ruby lips
> When he is gone?
> Look away—
> Look away—
> Over yonder!

(ACTORS *enter during this song and take their places in the dark.*)

TAPED: (ACTOR ONE *and underscored by* GIRL *with* "HE'S GONE AWAY").

THE HILL

Where are Elmer, Herman, Bert, Tom and Charley,
The weak of will, the strong of arm, the clown, the boozer, the fighter?
All, all, are sleeping on the hill.

One passed in a fever,
One was burned in a mine,
One was killed in a brawl,
One died in jail,
One fell from a bridge toiling for children and wife—
All, all are sleeping, sleeping, sleeping on the hill.

Where are Ella, Kate, Mag, Lizzie and Edith,
The tender heart, the simple soul, the loud, the proud,
   the happy one?—
All, all are sleeping on the hill.

One died in shameful child-birth,
One of a thwarted love,
One at the hands of a brute in a brothel,
One of a broken pride, in the search for heart's desire,
One after life in far-away London and Paris
Was brought to her little space by Ella and Kate and
   Mag—
All, all are sleeping, sleeping, sleeping on the hill.

(*LIGHTS up bright on Area 1.*)

TOM BEATTY (ACTOR ONE)
(*Laughs.*)
And I say to you that Life's a gambler
Head and shoulders above us all.
No mayor alive can close the house.
And if you lose, you can squeal as you will;
You'll not get back your money.
He makes the percentage hard to conquer;
He stacks the cards to catch your weakness
And not to meet your strength.
And he gives you seventy years to play:
For if you cannot win in seventy
You cannot win at all.
So, if you lose, get out of the room—
Get out of the room when your time is up.
It's mean to sit and fumble the cards,
And curse your losses, leaden-eyed,
Whining to try and try.
(*Laughs.*)

(*LIGHTS comes up full and stay that way through "Deacon Taylor."*)

ILLINOIS—SONG (*Both singers*)

BOY.

> Way down upon the Wabash
> Such land was never known.
> If Adam had crossed over it,
> This soil he'd surely own.

GIRL.

> He'd swear it was the garden
> He played in as a boy,
> And straight pronounce it Eden

BOTH.

> In the state of Illinois.

GIRL.

> It's bounded by the Wabash
> The Missouri and the lakes.

BOY.

> There's quicksand in her swampy land
> And in her fields are snakes,

GIRL.

> But these are just diversions
> That take not from the joy

BOTH.

> Of living in the garden spot—
> The state of Illinois.
> So move your family westward,
> Good health you will enjoy,
> And rise to wealth and honor
> In the state of Illinois—
> The state of Illinois—
> The state of Illinois!

MRS. WILLIAMS (ACTRESS TWO)

I was the milliner,
Talked about, lied about,
Mother of Dora,
Whose strange appearance
Was charged to her rearing.
My eye quick to beauty
Saw much beside ribbons

And buckles and feathers
And leghorns and felts,
To set off sweet faces,
And dark hair and gold.
One thing I will tell you
And one I will ask:
The stealers of husbands
Wear powder and trinkets,
And fashionable hats.
Wives, wear them yourselves.
Hats may make divorces—
They also prevent them.
Well now, let me ask you:
If all of the children, born here in Spoon River
Had been reared by the County, somewhere on a farm;
And the fathers and mothers had been given their free-
    dom
To live and enjoy, change mates if they wished,
Do you think that Spoon River
Had been any the worse?

DORA WILLIAMS (ACTRESS FOUR)
When Reuben Pantier ran away and threw me
I went to Springfield. There I met a lush,
Whose father, just deceased, left him a fortune.
He married me when drunk. My life was wretched.
A year passed and one day they found him dead.
That made me rich. I moved on to Chicago.
After a time met Tyler Rountree, villain.
I moved on to New York. A gray-haired magnate
Went mad about me—so another fortune.
He died one night right in my arms, you know.
(I saw his purple face for years thereafter.)
There was almost a scandal. I moved on,
This time to Paris. I was now a woman,
Insidious, subtle, versed in the world and rich.
My sweet apartment near the Champs Elysées
Became a center for all sorts of people,
Musicians, poets, dandies, artists, nobles,

Where we spoke French and German, Italian, English.
I wed Count Navigato, native of Genoa.
We went to Rome. He poisoned me, I think.
Now in the Camp Santo overlooking
The sea where young Columbus dreamed new worlds,
See what they chiseled: *"Contessa Navigato
Implora eterna quiete."*

ARCHIBALD HIGBIE (ACTOR THREE)
I loathed you, Spoon River. I tried to rise above you,
I was ashamed of you. I despised you
As the place of my nativity.
And there in Rome, among the artists,
Speaking Italian, speaking French,
I seemed to myself at times to be free
Of every trace of my origin.
I seemed to be reaching the heights of art
And to breathe the air that the masters breathed,
And to see the world with their eyes.
But still they'd pass my work and say:
"What are you driving at, my friend?
Sometimes the face looks like Apollo's,
At others it has a trace of Lincoln's."
There was no culture, you know, in Spoon River,
And I burned with shame and held my peace.
And what could I do, all covered over
And weighted down with western soil,
Except aspire, and pray for another
Birth in the world, with all of Spoon River
Rooted out of my soul?

WALTER SIMMONS (ACTOR ONE)
My parents thought that I would be
As great as Edison or greater:
For as a boy I made balloons
And wondrous kites and toys with clocks
And little engines with tracks to run on
And telephones of cans and thread.
I played the cornet and painted pictures,

(GIRL SINGER
*underscores,
humming and
playing "I
AM, I AM."*)

Modeled in clay and took the part
Of the villain in "The Octoroon."
But then at twenty-one I married
And had to live, and so, to live
I learned the trade of making watches
And kept the jewelry store on the square,
Thinking, thinking, thinking, thinking—
Not of business, but of the engine
I studied the calculus to build.
And all Spoon River watched and waited
To see it work, but it never worked.
And a few kind souls believed my genius
Was somehow hampered by the store.
It wasn't true. The truth was this:
I didn't have the brains.

(GIRL SINGER underscores, humming and playing "I AM, I AM.")

DEACON TAYLOR (ACTOR THREE)
I BELONGED to the church,
And to the party of prohibition;
And the villagers thought I died of eating watermelon.
In truth I had cirrhosis of the liver,
For every noon for thirty years,
I slipped behind the prescription partition
In Trainor's drug store
And poured a generous drink
From the bottle marked
"Spiritus frumenti."

*(Cross-fade—general LIGHTING out to light on AC-
    TRESS FOUR.)*

EMILY SPARKS (ACTRESS FOUR)
Only the chemist can tell, and not always the chemist
What will result from compounding
Fluids or solids.
And who can tell
How men and women will interact
On each other, or what children will result?

There were Benjamin Pantier and his wife,
Good in themselves, but evil toward each other:
He oxygen, she hydrogen,
Their son, a devastating fire.

(LIGHTS intro-duce ACTORS *and they rise and come forward as they are intro-duced by* EMILY SPARKS.)

(MALE SINGER *underscores on guitar with "SPOON RIVER" music.*)

BENJAMIN PANTIER (ACTOR ONE)
Together in this grave lie Benjamin Pantier, Attorney at
    Law
And Nig, his dog, constant companion, solace and friend.
Down the gray road, friends, children, men and women,
Passing one by one out of life, left me till I was alone
With Nig for partner, bed-fellow, comrade in drink.
In the morning of life I knew aspiration and saw glory.
Then she, who survives me, snared my soul
With a snare which bled me to death.
Till I, once strong of will, lay broken, indifferent,
Living with Nig in a room back of a dingy office.

MRS. BENJAMIN PANTIER (ACTRESS TWO)
I know that he told that I snared his soul
With a snare which bled him to death.
And all the men loved him,
And most of the women pitied him.
But suppose you are really a lady, and have delicate
    tastes,
And loathe the smell of whiskey and onions.
And the rhythm of Wordsworth ode runs in your ears,
While he goes about from morning till night
Repeating bits of that common thing:
"Oh, why should the spirit of mortal be proud?"
And then, suppose:
You are a woman well endowed,
And the only man with whom the law and morality

Permit you to have the marital relation
Is the very man that fills you with disgust
Every time you think of it—while you think of it
Every time you see him?
That's why I drove him away from home
To live with his dog in a dingy room
Back of his office.

BENJAMIN PANTIER (ACTOR ONE)
Under my jaw-bone is snuggled the bony nose of Nig
Our story is lost in silence. Go by, mad world!

(ACTOR ONE *and* ACTRESS TWO *look at each other briefly.
Their LIGHTS go out. They return to their benches.*)

(ACTOR THREE *moves behind* ACTRESS FOUR *who is
seated on her bench.*)

EMILY SPARKS (ACTRESS FOUR)
Where is my boy, my boy—
In what far part of the world?
The boy I loved best of all in the world?—
I, the teacher, the old maid, the virgin heart,
Who made them all my children.
Did I know my boy aright,
Thinking of him as spirit aflame,
Active, ever aspiring?

REUBEN PANTIER (ACTOR THREE)
Well, Emily Sparks, your prayers were not wasted,
Your love was not all in vain.
I owe whatever I was in life
To your hope that would not give me up,
To your love that saw me still as good.
Dear Emily Sparks, let me tell you the story.
I pass the effect of my father and mother;
The milliner's daughter made me trouble
And out I went in the world,
Where I passed through every peril known

Of wine and women and joy of life.
One night, in a room in the Rue de Rivoli,
I was drinking wine with a black-eyed cocotte,
And the tears swam into my eyes.
She thought they were amorous tears and smiled
For thought of her conquest over me.
But my soul was three thousand miles away,
In the days when you taught me in Spoon River.
And just because you no more could love me,
Nor pray for me, nor write me letters,
The eternal silence of you spoke instead.
And the black-eyed cocotte took the tears for hers,
As well as the deceiving kisses I gave her.
Somehow, from that hour, I had a new vision—
Dear Emily Sparks!

EMILY SPARKS (ACTRESS TWO)
Oh, boy, boy, for whom I prayed and
    prayed
In many a watchful hour at night,
Do you remember the letter I wrote you   (MALE
Of the beautiful love of Christ?   SINGER
And whether you ever took it or not,   *underscores*
My boy, wherever you are,   *with*
Work for your soul's sake,   *"SPOON*
That all the clay of you, all of the dross of *RIVER"*
    you   *music.*)
May yield to the fire of you,
Till the fire is nothing but light!
Nothing but light!

(*LIGHT goes out. ACTOR THREE returns to his bench.*)

MARGARET FULLER SLACK (ACTRESS TWO)
I would have been as great as George Eliot
But for an untoward fate.
For look at the photograph of me made by Penniwit,
Chin resting on hand, and deep-set eyes—
Gray, too, and far-searching.

But there was the old, old problem:
Should it be celibacy, matrimony or unchastity?
Then John Slack, the rich druggist, wooed me,
Luring me with the promise of leisure for my novel,
And I married him, giving birth to eight children,
And had no time to write.
It was all over with me, anyway,
When I ran the needle in my hand
While washing the baby's things,
And died from lock-jaw, an ironical death.
Hear me, ambitious souls,
Sex is the curse of life!

(Cross-fade to Area 7 LIGHT.)

SOLDIER OH SOLDIER—SONG (MALE SINGER)
>Soldier oh soldier,
>A comin' from the plain,
>Courted fair lady
>Though he didn't know her name.
>Her beauty shone so bright
>That it didn't seem to matter,
>And he'd kiss her on the mouth
>Just to stop her endless chatter.
>Fa la la la—
>Fa la la la—
>Fa la la la—
>Fa la la la!

(Cross-fade to Area 1.)

KNOWLT HOHEIMER (ACTOR ONE)
I was the first fruits of the battle of Missionary Ridge.
When I felt the bullet enter my heart
I wished I had stayed at home and gone to jail
For stealing the hogs of Curl Trenary,
Instead of running away and joining the army.
Rather a thousand times the county jail
Than to lie under this marble figure with wings,

And this granite pedestal
Bearing the words, *"Pro Patria."*
What do they mean, anyway?

(*Cross-fade to Area 4.*)

LYDIA PUCKETT (ACTRESS FOUR)
Knowlt Hoheimer ran away to the war
The day before Curl Trenary
Swore out a warrant through Justice Arnett
For stealing hogs.
But that's not the reason he turned a soldier.
He caught me running with Lucius Atherton.
We quarreled and I told him never again
To cross my path.
Then he stole the hogs and went to the war—
Back of every soldier is a woman.

(*BLACKOUT.*)

(*LIGHTS up full. Square dance:* ACTOR THREE *and* AC-
TRESS TWO *dance to "SKIP T'MY LOU." It is
played on fiddle by* GIRL SINGER *and on banjo by*
MALE SINGER.)

FIDDLER JONES (ACTOR THREE)
The earth keeps some vibration going
There in your heart, and that is you.
And if the people find you can fiddle,
Why, fiddle you must, for all your life.
How could I till my forty acres
Not to speak of getting more,
With a medley of horns, bassoons and piccolos
Stirred in my brain by crows and robins
And the creak of a wind-mill-only these?
And I never started to plow in my life
That some one did not stop in the road
And take me away to a dance or picnic.
I ended up with forty acres;

I ended up with a broken fiddle—
And a broken laugh and a thousand memories,
And not a single regret.

(*BLACKOUT.*)

(ACTOR ONE *and* ACTRESS FOUR *each move forward in
their areas. The LIGHTS are cold on them.*)

OLLIE McGEE (ACTRESS FOUR)
Have you seen walking through the village
A man with downcast eyes and haggard face?
That is my husband who, by secret cruelty
Never to be told, robbed me of my youth and my beauty;
Till at last, wrinkled and with yellow teeth,
And with broken pride and shameful humility,
I sank into the grave.
But what think you gnaws at my husband's heart?
The face of what I was, the face of what he made me!
These are driving him to the place where I lie.
In death, therefore, I am avenged.

FLETCHER McGEE (ACTOR TWO)
She took my strength by minutes,
She took my life by hours,
She drained me like a fevered moon
That saps the spinning world.
The days went by like shadows,
The minutes wheeled like stars.
She took the pity from my heart,
And made it into smiles.
She was a hunk of sculptor's clay,
My secret thoughts were fingers:
They flew behind her pensive brow
And lined it deep with pain.
They set the lips, and sagged the cheeks,
And drooped the eyes with sorrow.
My soul had entered in the clay,
Fighting like seven devils.

It was not mine, it was not hers;
She held it, but its struggles
Modeled a face she hated,
And a face I feared to see.
I beat the windows, shook the bolts.
I hid me in a corner—
And then she died* and haunted me,
And hunted me for life.

*(They stare at each other while returning to their benches
as the LIGHTS fade out.)*

(CROWD noises.)

ACTOR ONE.
    And now! Judge . . .
    Leader in the state . . .
    Member of Congress . . .
    Hamilton Greene!!!

(CROWD cheers and applauds.)

HAMILTON GREENE—ELSA WERTMAN

GREENE (ACTOR THREE)
(Goes to lectern.)
Do you remember when I fought the bank and the
Courthouse ring, for pocketing the interest on
Public funds?
And when I fought our leading citizens for making
The poor the pack horses of the taxes?
And when I fought the business men who fought me
In these fights?
Then do you remember?

WERTMAN (ACTRESS TWO)
I was a peasant girl from Germany,
Blue-eyed, rosy, happy and strong.

* Guitar sting.

And the first place I worked was at the Thomas Greenes.
On a summer's day when she was away he stole into the
Kitchen and took me right in his arms and kissed me
On my throat, I turning my head. Then neither of us
Seemed to know what happened. And I cried for what
Would become of me.
And I cried and cried as my secret began to show.
One day Mrs. Greene said she understood, and would
Make no trouble for me, and, being childless, would
Adopt it. (He had given her a farm to be still.)
So she hid in the house and sent out rumors, as if it were
Going to happen to her. And all went well and the child
Was born—they were so kind to me.

GREENE (ACTOR THREE)

I was the only child of Frances Harris of Virginia
And Thomas Greene of Kentucky, of valiant and honor-
    able
Blood both. From my mother I inherited vivacity,
Fancy, language; from my father will, judgment, logic.
All honor to them for what service I was to the people.

WERTMAN (ACTRESS TWO)

But—at political rallies when sitters-by thought I
Was crying at the eloquence of Hamilton Greene—
That was not it.
No! I wanted to say:
That's my son! That's my son!

ROSIE ROBERTS (ACTRESS FOUR)

I was sick, but more than that, I was mad
At the crooked police, and the crooked game of life.
So I wrote to the Chief of Police at Peoria:
"I am here in my girlhood home in Spoon River,
Gradually wasting away.
But come and take me, I killed the son
Of the merchant prince, in Madam Lou's,
And the papers that said he killed himself
In his home while cleaning a hunting gun—

Lied like the devil to hush up scandal,
For the bribe of advertising.
In my room I shot him, at Madam Lou's,
Because he knocked me down when I said
That, in spite of all the money he had,
I'd see my lover that night."

(*During this speech she comes forward in her area and
has collapsed Downstage by the end of the poem.*)

RUSSIAN SONIA (ACTRESS TWO)

I, born in Weimar
Of a mother who was French
And German father, a most learned professor,
Orphaned at fourteen years,
Became a dancer, known as Russian Sonia,
All up and down the boulevards of Paris,
Mistress betimes of sundry dukes and counts,
And later of poor artists and of poets.
At forty years, *passee*, I sought New York
And met old Patrick Hummer on the boat,
Red-faced and hale, though turned his sixtieth year,
Returning after having sold a ship-load
Of cattle in the German city, Hamburg.
He brought me to Spoon River and we lived here
For twenty years—they thought that we were married!
This oak tree near me is the favorite haunt
Of blue jays chattering, chattering all the day.
And why not? for my very dust is laughing
For thinking of the humorous thing called life.

(*She ends Downstage in her area.*)

LUCIUS ATHERTON (ACTOR THREE)

When my moustache curled,
And my hair was black,
And I wore tight trousers
And a diamond stud,
I was an excellent knave of hearts
   and took many a trick.

(*He moves over to
ACTRESS TWO and
flirts. He's rejected
and ACTRESS TWO
goes back to her
bench.*)

But when the gray hairs began to appear—
Lo! a new generation of girls
Laughed at me, not fearing me,
And I had no more exciting adventures
Wherein I was all but shot for a heartless
   devil,
But only drabby affairs, warmed-over
   affairs
Of other days and other men.

(He moves to ACTRESS FOUR *and she moves back to her bench.)*

And time went on until I lived at Mayer's
   restaurant,
Partaking of short-orders, a gray, untidy,
Toothless, discarded, rural Don Juan . . .
There is a mighty shade here, Dante, who
   sings
Of one named Beatrice;
And I see now that the force that made
   him great
Drove me to the dregs of life.

*(*GIRL SINGER *hums* "TIMES ARE GETTIN' HARD, BOYS.")*

TIMES ARE GETTIN' HARD, BOYS—SONG
(GIRL SINGER)

Times are gettin' hard, boys,
Money's gettin' scarce.
If times don't get no better, boys,
Bound to leave this place.
Take my true love by the hand,
Walk right through the town,
Tellin' friends we're goin' away,
That we're goin' away.

EUGENE CARMEN (ACTOR ONE)

Rhodes' slave! Selling shoes and gingham,
Flour and bacon, overalls, clothing, all
   day long
For fourteen hours a day for three hun-
   dred and thirteen days
For more than twenty years,
Saying "Yes'm" and "Yes, sir" and
   "Thank you"

*(*GIRL SINGER *humming* "TIMES ARE GETTIN' HARD, BOYS.")*

A thousand times a day, and all for fifty
   dollars a month.
Living in this stinking room in the rattle-
   trap "Commercial."
And compelled to go to Sunday School,
   and to listen
To the Rev. Abner Peet one hundred and
   four times a year
For more than an hour at a time,
Because Thomas Rhodes ran the church
As well as the store and the bank.

(GIRL SINGER *humming* "TIMES ARE GETTIN' HARD, BOYS.")

So while I was tying my neck-tie that morning
I suddenly saw myself in the glass:
My hair all gray, my face like a sodden pie.
So I cursed and cursed: You damned old thing!
You cowardly dog! You rotten pauper!
You Rhodes' slave! Till Roger Baugham
Thought I was having a fight with someone,
And looked through the transom just in time
To see me fall on the floor in a heap
From a broken vein in my head.

THE WATER IS WIDE—SONG (*Both singers*)

The water is wide,
And we cannot get o'er,
And neither have we
Wings to fly.
Give us a boat
That can carry two
And both shall vow,
My love and I.

(GIRL SINGER.)

Down in the meadows
The other day,
A gatherin' flowers both fine and gay,
A gatherin' flowers of red and blue,
We'd give a thought to what love can do.

(GIRL SINGER *with humming by* MALE SINGER.)

(*During these two verses* ACTRESS TWO *and* ACTOR

THREE *meet in front of lectern. They move Down Center, turn and face each other. Then they kiss.*)

WILLIAM & EMILY (ACTOR THREE *and* ACTRESS TWO)
WILLIAM & EMILY
(ACTOR THREE *and* ACTRESS TWO)
(*Humming of "WATER IS WIDE" throughout*)
BOTH.

There is something about death
EMILY.

Like love itself!
WILLIAM.

If with someone with whom you have known passion,
EMILY.

And the glow of youthful love,
WILLIAM.

You also
EMILY.

After years of life together
WILLIAM.

Feel the sinking of the fire,
EMILY.

And thus fade away together . . . gradually—

WILLIAM.	EMILY.
Faintly—	Delicately—

WILLIAM.

As it were in each other's arms.
EMILY.

Passing from the familiar room
BOTH.

That is a power of unison
Between souls/ Like love itself.

WATER IS WIDE—SONG
(GIRL SINGER *and* MALE SINGER)

Our love was handsome,   (ACTORS *kiss, walk back to*
Our love was fine,   *lectern arm in arm and slip*
Our love was like a ruby   *back to their benches as*
When it is new.   *LIGHT fades out.*)

As our love grew old,   ) (ACTORS *kiss, walk back to*
It sparkled true,   (*lectern arm in arm and slip*
It did not fade   (*back to their benches as*
It only grew.   ) *LIGHT fades out.*)

YEE BOW (ACTRESS FOUR)

(*Oriental intro. by* MALE SINGER *on guitar*)

They got me into the Sunday School
In Spoon River
And tried to get me to drop Confucius for Jesus.
I could have been no worse off
If I had tried to get them to drop Jesus for Confucius.
For, without any warning, as if it were a prank,
And sneaking up behind me, Harry Wiley,
The minister's son, caved my ribs into my lungs,
With a blow of his fist.
Now I shall never sleep with my ancestors in Pekin,
And no children shall worship at my grave.

(*Oriental exit by* MALE SINGER *on guitar.*)

(*CROWD hisses and boos.*)

ENOCH DUNLAP (ACTOR ONE)

(*At lectern.*)

How many times, during the twenty years
I was your leader, friends of Spoon River,
Did you neglect the convention and caucus,
And leave the burden on my hands
Of guarding and saving the people's cause? (*CROWD boos.*)
Sometimes because you were ill;
Or your grandmother was ill;
Or you drank too much and fell asleep;
Or else you said: "He is our leader,

All will be well; he fights for us;
We have nothing to do but follow." (*CROWD boos.*)
But oh, how you cursed me when I fell,
And cursed me, saying I had betrayed you,
In leaving the caucus room for a moment,
When the people's enemies, there assembled,
Waited and watched for a chance to destroy
The Sacred Rights of the People. (*CROWD boos.*)
You common rabble! I left the caucus
To go to the urinal!

MRS. KESSLER (ACTRESS TWO)

Mr. Kessler, you know, was in the army,
And he drew six dollars a month as a pension,
And stood on the corner talking politics,
Or sat at home reading Grant's memoirs;
And I supported the family by washing,
Learning the secrets of all the people
From their curtains, counterpanes, shirts and skirts.
For things that are new grow old at length,
They're replaced with better or none at all:
People are prospering or falling back.
And rents and patches widen with time;
No thread or needle can pace decay,
And there are stains that baffle soap,
And there are colors that run in spite of you,
Blamed though you are for spoiling a dress.
Handkerchiefs, napery, have their secrets—
The laundress, Life, knows all about it.
And I, who went to all the funerals
Held in Spoon River, swear I never
Saw a dead face without thinking it looked
Like something washed and ironed.

NANCY KNAPP (ACTRESS FOUR)

Well, don't you see, this was the way of it:
We bought the farm with what he inherited,

And his brothers and sisters accused him of poisoning
His father's mind against the rest of them.
And we never had any peace with our treasure.
The murrain took the cattle, and the crops failed.
And lightning struck the granary.
So we mortgaged the farm to keep going.
And he grew silent and was worried all the time.
Then some of the neighbors refused to speak to us,
And took sides with his brothers and sisters.
And I had no place to turn, as one may say to himself,
At an earlier time in life; "No matter,
So and so is my friend, or I can shake this off
With a little trip to Decatur."
Then the dreadfulest smells infested the rooms.
So I set fire to the beds and the old witch-house
Went up in a roar of flames,
As I danced in the yard with waving arms,
While he wept like a freezing steer.

GEORGE GRAY (ACTOR ONE)

(*Still at lectern.*)
I have studied many times
The marble which was chiseled for me—
A boat with a furled sail at rest in a harbor.
In truth it pictures not my destination
But my life.
For love was offered me and I shrank from its disillu-
    sionment;
Sorrow knocked at my door, but I was afraid;
Ambition called to me, but I dreaded the chances.
Yet all the while I hungered for meaning in my life.
And now I know that we must lift the sail
And catch the winds of destiny
Wherever they drive the boat.
To put meaning in one's life may end in madness,
But life without meaning is the torture
Of restlessness and vague desire—
It is a boat longing for the sea and yet afraid.

(SINGERS *whistle first four bars of "WHEN JOHNNY COMES MARCHING HOME."*)

HARRY WILMANS (ACTOR THREE)
I was just turned twenty-one,
And Henry Phipps, the Sunday-school superintendent,
Made a speech in Bindle's Opera House.

ACTOR ONE
(*At lectern.*)
The honor of the flag must be upheld whether it be
Assailed by a barbarous tribe of Tagalogs, or the
Greatest power in Europe.

(EVERYONE *waves small American flags.*)

HARRY WILMANS (ACTOR THREE)
And we cheered and cheered the speech and the flag
He waved as he spoke. And I went to the war in spite
Of my father. And followed the flag until I saw it
Raised by our camp in a rice field near Manila, and all
Of us cheered and cheered it.
But there were flies and poisonous things: and there was
The deadly water, and the cruel heat, and the sickening
Putrid food: and the smell of the trench just back of the
Tents where the soldiers went to empty themselves. And
There were the whores who followed us, full of syphilis.
And beastly acts between ourselves or alone, with bullying
Hated, degradation among us, and days of loathing, and
Nights of fear to the hour of the charge through the
Steaming swamp, following the flag.
Till I fell, with a scream,
Shot through the guts.
Now there's a flag over me in Spoon River, a flag!
  (EVERYONE *raises their flags.*) A flag!

(ALL *whistle last four bars of "JOHNNY COMES MARCHING HOME." During whistling,* ACTOR ONE *marches back to his bench.*)

NELLIE CLARK (ACTRESS TWO)

I was only eight years old:
And before I grew up and knew what it
    meant
I had no words for it, except
That I was frightened and told my
    Mother;
And that my Father got a pistol
And would have killed Charlie, who was
    a big boy,
Fifteen years old, except for his Mother.
Nevertheless the story clung to me.
But the man who married me, a widower
    of thirty-five,
Was a newcomer and never heard it
Till two years after we were married.
Then he considered himself cheated,
And the village agreed that I was not really a virgin.
Well, he deserted me, and I died
The following winter.

(MALE SINGER
*underscores
on guitar with
"JIMMY
CRACK
CORN."*)

PAPER OF PINS—SONG (*Both singers*)

BOY.

I'll give to you a paper of pins,
To show you how our love begins,
If you will marry, marry me,
If you will marry me.

GIRL.

I'll not accept your paper of pins
To show me how our love begins,
No I'll not marry you.
I'll not marry you.

BOY.

I'll give to you the keys to my heart,
So you can lock and never part,
If you will marry, marry me.
If you will marry me.

GIRL.

I'll not accept the keys to your heart,
So we can lock and never part,

No I'll not marry you,
I'll not marry you.
BOY.
   I'll give to you the keys to my chest,
   So you can have money at your request,
   If you will marry, marry me,
   If you will marry me.
GIRL.
   I will accept the keys to your chest,
   So I can have money at my request,
   Yes I'll marry you, you, you,
   Yes I'll marry you.

ROSCOE PURKAPILE (ACTOR ONE)

She loved me. Oh! how she loved me!
I never had a chance to escape
From the day she first saw me.
But then after we were married I thought
She might prove her mortality and let me out,
Or she might divorce me.
But few die, none resign.
Then I ran away and was gone a year on a lark.
But she never complained. She said all would be well,
That I would return. And I did return.
I told her that while taking a row in a boat
I had been captured near Van Buren Street
By pirates on Lake Michigan,
And kept in chains, so I could not write her.
She cried and kissed me, and said it was cruel,
Outrageous, inhuman!
I then concluded our marriage
Was a divine dispensation
And could not be dissolved,
Except by death.
I was right.

MRS. PURKAPILE (ACTRESS FOUR)

He ran away and was gone for a year.
When he came home he told me the silly story
Of being kidnapped by pirates on Lake Michigan

And kept in chains so he could not write me.
I pretended to believe it, though I knew very well
What he was doing, and that he met
The milliner, Mrs. Williams, now and then
When she went to the city to buy goods, as she said.
But a promise is a promise
And marriage is marriage,
And out of respect for my own character
I refused to be drawn into a divorce
By the scheme of a husband who had merely grown tired
Of his marital vow and duty.

A. D. Blood (Actor Three)
If you in the village think that my work was a good one,
Who closed the saloons and stopped all playing at cards,
And haled old Daisy Fraser before Justice Arnett,
In many a crusade to purge the people of sin;
Why do you let the milliner's daughter, Dora,
And the worthless son of Benjamin Pantier
Nightly make my grave their unholy pillow?

Shack Dye (Actor One)
The white men played all sorts of jokes on
    me.
They took big fish off my hook
And put little ones on, while I was away
Getting a stringer, and made me believe
I hadn't seen aright the fish I had caught.
When Burr Robbins' circus came to town
They got the ringmaster to let a tame
    leopard
Into the ring, and made me believe
I was whipping a wild beast like Samson
When I for an offer of fifty dollars,
Dragged him out to his cage.
One time I entered my blacksmith shop
And shook as I saw some horse-shoes
    crawling
Across the floor, as if alive—
Walter Simmons had put a magnet
Under the barrel of water.

(Girl
Singer
hums
"FREE-
DOM.")

Yet every one of you, you white men,
Was fooled about fish and about leopards too,
And you didn't know any more than the horse-shoes did
What moved you about Spoon River.

FREEDOM—SONG (MALE SINGER)
    Long time a comin',
    Oh Lord,
    Long time a comin',
    Dear Lord,
    Long time a comin',
    Please, dear Lord,
    I want freedom now, oh Lord,
    I want freedom now.

    I pray for freedom,
    Oh Lord,
    I pray for freedom,
    Dear Lord,
    I pray for freedom,
    Please, dear Lord,
    I want freedom now, oh Lord,
    I want freedom now.

HANNAH ARMSTRONG (ACTRESS FOUR)
(GIRL SINGER *hums "IN THE NIGHT" throughout*.)
I wrote him a letter asking him for old times' sake
To discharge my sick boy from the army.
But maybe he couldn't read it.
Then I went to town and had James Garber,
Who wrote beautifully, write him a letter;
But maybe that was lost in the mails.
So I traveled all the way to Washington.
I was more than an hour finding the White House.
And when I found it they turned me away,
Hiding their smiles. Then I thought:
"Oh, well, he ain't the same as when I boarded him
And he and my husband worked together
And all of us called him Abe, there in Menard."

As a last attempt I turned to a guard and said:
"Please say it's old Aunt Hannah Armstrong
From Illinois, come to see him about her sick boy
In the army."
Well, just in a moment they let me in!
And when he saw me he broke in a laugh,
And dropped his business as President,
And wrote in his hand Doug's discharge,
Talking the while of the early days,
And telling stories.

(SINGERS *play and hum "WHO KNOWS WHERE I'M
GOING?"*)

FAITH MATHENY (ACTRESS TWO)
(*She moves Down Center.*)
At first you will know not what they mean,
And you may never know,
And we may never tell you:—
These sudden flashes in your soul,
Like lambent lightning on snowy clouds
At midnight when the moon is full.
They come in solitude, or perhaps
You sit with your friend, and all at once
A silence falls on speech, and his eyes
Without a flicker glow at you:—
You two have seen the secret together,
He sees it in you, and you in him,
And there you sit thrilling lest the Mystery
Stand before you and strike you dead
With a splendor like the sun's.
Be brave, all souls who have such visions!
As your body's alive as mine is dead,
You're catching a little whiff of the ether
Reserved for God Himself.

(*The rest
of the
CAST rises
and moves
forward,
joining
hands with
ACTRESS
TWO.*)

(ALL *unclasp hands, spread out slightly and bow. Then
they exit.*)

END OF ACT ONE

ACT TWO

The LIGHTS come up full. The ACTORS *walk on Stage, stand at their benches and bow. Then they sit.*

THREE NIGHTS DRUNK—SONG (*Both singers*)

BOY.

The first night that I came home so drunk
I couldn't see,
I found a horse in the stable where my horse
Ought to be.
Come here my little wife and explain this thing
To me. How come a horse in the stable
Where my horse ought to be?

GIRL.

You blind fool, you crazy fool, can't you never see?
It's only a milk cow your friend sent to me.

BOY.

I've travelled this world over 10,000 miles or more
But a saddle upon a milk cow's back, I never did
See before.
The second night that I came home so drunk I
Couldn't see,
I found a coat a hangin' on the rack where my
Coat ought to be

GIRL.

You blind fool, you crazy fool, can't you never see?
It's only a bed quilt your friend sent to me.

BOY.

I've travelled this world over 10,000 miles or more
But pockets upon a bed quilt
I never did see before
Third night that I came home so drunk I couldn't
See,
I found a head a layin' on the pillow where my
Head ought to be.

34

GIRL.

    You blind fool, you crazy fool, can't you never
    See?
    It's only a cabbage head your friend sent to me.

BOY.

    I've travelled this world over 10,000 miles or
    More
    But a mustache on a cabbage head
    I never did see before.

JUDGE SELAH LIVELY (ACTOR ONE)

(*On his knees behind his bench.*)

Suppose you stood just five feet two,
And had worked your way as a grocery clerk,
Studying law by candlelight
Until you became an attorney at law?
And then suppose through your diligence,
And regular church attendance,
You became attorney for Thomas Rhodes,
Collecting notes and mortgages,
And representing all the widows
In the Probate Court? And through it all
They jeered at your size, and laughed at your clothes
And your polished boots? And then suppose
You became the County Judge?
And Jefferson Howard and Kinsey Keene,
And Harmon Whitney, and all the giants
Who had sneered at you, were forced to stand
Before the bar and say "Your Honor"—
Well, don't you think it was natural
That I made it hard for them?

ZILPHA MARSH (ACTRESS FOUR)

At four o'clock in late October
I sat alone in the country school house
Back from the road mid stricken fields,
And an eddy of wind blew leaves on the pane,
And crooned in the flue of the cannon stove,
With its open door blurring the shadows

With the spectral glow of a dying fire.
In an idle mood I was running the planchette—
All at once my wrist grew limp,
And my hand moved rapidly over the board,
Till the name "Charles Giuteau" was spelled,
Who threatened to materialize before me.
I rose and fled from the room bare-headed into the dusk,
Afraid of my gift.
After that the spirits swarmed—Chaucer, Caesar, Poe and
Marlowe, Cleopatra and Mrs. Surrat—wherever I went,
    with messages—

ACTOR ONE
Mere trifling twaddle—

ACTRESS TWO
Charles Guiteau indeed!

ACTOR THREE
You talk nonsense to children—

MARSH
And suppose I see what you never saw and never heard of
And have no word for,
I must talk nonsense when you ask me what it is I see!

SEARCY FOOTE (ACTOR THREE)
I wanted to go away to college
But rich Aunt Persis wouldn't help me.
So I made gardens and raked the lawns
And bought John Alden's books with my earnings
And toiled for the very means of life.
I wanted to marry Delia Prickett,
But how could I do it with what I earned?
And there was Aunt Persis more than seventy,
Who sat in a wheel-chair half alive,
With her throat so paralyzed, when she swallowed
The soup ran out of her mouth like a duck—
A gourmand yet, investing her income

In mortgages, fretting all the time
About her notes and rents and papers.
That day I was sawing wood for her,
And reading Proudhon in between.
I went in the house for a drink of water,
And there she sat asleep in her chair,
And Proudhon lying on the table,
And a bottle of chloroform on the book,
She used sometimes for an aching tooth!
I poured the chloroform on a handkerchief
And held it to her nose till she died.—
Oh, Delia, Delia, you and Proudhon
Steadied my hand, and the coroner
Said she died of heart failure.
I married Delia and got the money—
A joke on you, Spoon River?

MRS. CHARLES BLISS (ACTRESS TWO)
Reverend Wiley advised me not to divorce him
For the sake of the children,
And Judge Somers advised him the same.
So we stuck to the end of the path.
But two of the children thought he was right,
And two of the children thought I was right.
And the two who sided with him blamed me,
And the two who sided with me blamed him,
And they grieved for the one they sided with.
And all were torn with the guilt of judging,
And tortured in soul because they could not admire
Equally him and me.
Now every gardener knows that plants grown in cellars
Or under stones are twisted and yellow and weak.
And no mother would let her baby suck
Diseased milk from her breast.
Yet preachers and judges advise the raising of souls
Where there is no sunlight, but only twilight,
No warmth, but only dampness and cold—
Preachers and judges!

FAR AWAY FROM HOME—SONG (MALE SINGER)
Oh, the night it is cold,
And there's no one here to hold—
Far away, oh, so far from my home.
Gone away, gone to stay,
For a thousand lonely days,
I'm so far, oh, so far from my home.

Through these eyes all I see
Is a lot of misery,
Far away, oh, so far from my home—
God, the silence is hell
And I feel I want to yell—
I'm so far, oh, so far
From my home.

(*All* FOUR AC-
TORS *slowly come
Down Center.*
ACTOR THREE
*sits on apron of
Stage.* ACTRESS
TWO *kneels to
his left.* ACTOR
ONE *and* AC-
TRESS FOUR *stand
on either side of
them.*)

PAULINE BARRETT (ACTRESS FOUR)
Almost the shell of a woman after the surgeon's knife!
And almost a year to creep back into strength,
Till the dawn of our wedding decennial
Found me my seeming self again.
We walked the forest together,
By a path of soundless moss and turf.
But I could not look in your eyes,
And you could not look in my eyes,
For such sorrow was ours—the beginning of gray in your
     hair,
And I but a shell of myself.
And what did we talk of?—sky and water,
Anything, 'most, to hide our thoughts.
And then your gift of wild roses,
Set on the table to grace our dinner.
Poor heart, how bravely you struggled
To imagine and live a remembered rapture!
Then my spirit drooped as the night came on,

And you left me alone in my room for a while,
As you did when I was a bride, poor heart.
And I looked in the mirror and something said:
"One should be all dead when one is half-dead—"
Nor ever mock life, nor ever cheat love."
And I did it looking there in the mirror—
Dear, have you ever understood?

THE VILLAGE ATHEIST (ACTOR THREE)

Ye young debaters over the doctrine
Of the soul's immortality,
I who lie here was the village atheist,
Talkative, contentious, versed in the arguments
Of the infidels.
But through a long sickness
Coughing myself to death
I read the *Upanishads* and the poetry of Jesus.
And they lighted a torch of hope and intuition
And desire which the Shadow,
Leading me swiftly through the caverns of darkness,
Could not extinguish.
Listen to me, ye who live in the senses
And think through the senses only:
Immortality is not a gift,
Immortality is an achievement;
And only those who strive mightily
Shall possess it.

MABEL OSBORNE (ACTRESS TWO)

Your red blossoms amid green leaves
Are drooping, beautiful geranium!
But you do not ask for water.
You cannot speak! You do not need to speak—
Everyone knows that you are dying of thirst,
Yet they do not bring water!
They pass on, saying:
"The geranium wants water."
And I, who had happiness to share
And longed to share your happiness:
I who loved you, Spoon River,

And craved your love,
Withered before your eyes, Spoon River—
Thirsting, thirsting,
Voiceless from chasteness of soul to ask you for love,
You who knew and saw me perish before you,
Like this geranium which someone has planted over me,
And left to die.

FRANKLIN JONES (ACTOR ONE)

If I could have lived another year
I could have finished my flying machine,
And become rich and famous.
Hence it is fitting the workman
Who tried to chisel a dove for me
Made it look more like a chicken.
For what is it all but being hatched,
And running about the yard,
To the day of the block?
Save that a man has an angel's brain,
And sees the ax from the first!

SCHOFIELD HUXLEY (*Entire company*)

ACTOR ONE.

God . . .

ALL.

Ask us not to record your wonders, we admit
The stars and the suns and the countless
Worlds.

ACTOR THREE.

But we have measured their distances and weighed
Them and discovered their substances.

ACTOR ONE.

We have devised wings for the air

ACTOR THREE.

And keels for water

ACTOR ONE.

And horses of iron for the earth.

ACTRESS TWO.

We have lengthened the vision You gave us a
Million times,

ACTRESS FOUR.

And the hearing You gave us a million times.

ACTOR ONE.

We have leaped over space with speech

ACTOR THREE.

And taken fire for light out of the air.

ACTOR ONE.

We have built great cities and bored through
The hills and bridged majestic waters.

ACTOR THREE.

We have written the Iliad and Hamlet,

ACTRESS TWO.

And we have explored Your mysteries and searched
For You without ceasing.

ACTRESS FOUR.

And found You again after losing You in hours
Of weariness,

ALL.

And we ask You
How would You like to create a sun
And the next day
Have the worms
Slipping in and out
Between Your fingers?

(ACTOR ONE *and* ACTRESS FOUR *spread slightly and kneel.*)

IN THE NIGHT—SONG (GIRL SINGER)
(*STAR EFFECT on cyclorama*)
In the night
As I gaze
At the stars in their flight,
Seeking answers above,
Seeking all that is right.
Although nothing is said
In response to my plight,
I can see many things
That remain out of sight.

DIPPOLD THE OPTICIAN (*Entire company*)

ACTOR

or

ACTRESS:

1.   Try this lens . . . what do you see now?
2.   Globes of red, yellow, purple—
1.   Just a moment. And now?
2.   My father and mother and sisters.
1.   Yes. And now?
2.   Knights at arms, beautiful women, kind faces—
1.   Try this.
3.   A field of grain—a city.
1.   Very good! And now?
3.   A young woman with angels bending over her.
1.   A heavier lens. And now?
3.   Many women with bright eyes and open lips.
1.   Try this.
4.   Just a goblet on a table.
1.   Oh, I see. Try this lens.
4.   Just an open space—I see nothing in
      Particular.
1.   Well . . . and now?
4.   Pine trees, a lake, a summer sky.
1.   That's better. And now?
4.   A book.
1.   Read a page for me.
4.   I can't. My eyes are carried beyond the page.
1.   Try this lens.
ALL. Ooohh, depths of air.
1.   Excellent! And now?
ALL. Light, just light, making everything below it
      A toy world.
1.   Very well, we'll make the glasses accordingly.

IN THE NIGHT (GIRL SINGER)
(*Reprise*)
I can see
Many things
That remain out of sight.

ELIJAH BROWNING (ACTOR THREE)

I was among multitudes of children
Dancing at the foot of a mountain.
A breeze blew out of the east and swept them as
Leaves,
I arose and ascended higher, but a mist as from an
Iceberg
Clouded my steps. I was cold and in pain.
Then the sun streamed on me again,
And I saw the mists below me hiding all below them.
And above me,
Was the soundless air, pierced by a cone of ice,
Over which hung a solitary star!
A shudder of ecstasy, a shudder of fear
Ran through me. But I could not return to the slopes—
Nay, I wished not to return.
Therefore I climbed to the pinnacle.
I flung away my staff.
I touched that star
With my outstretched hand.
I vanished utterly.
For the mountain delivers to infinite truth
Whosoever touches the star!

MORNIN'S COME—SONG (*All singers*)

Mornin's come;
Night is past,
Stars have disappeared.
Sun will shine,
Darkness gone.
Now tomorrow's here.
All the fear of the night   \ (*The* ACTORS *slowly return to*
Melts away with dew.   / *their benches with the excep-*
Face the day;   > *tion of* ACTOR ONE *who ends*
Go your way,   \ *up in a standing position*
Seeking all that's true.   / *Downstage in Area 1.*)

ALEXANDER THROCKMORTON (ACTOR ONE)
In youth my wings were strong and tireless,

But I did not know the mountains.
In age I knew the mountains
But my weary wings could not follow my vision—
Genius is wisdom and youth.

AMANDA BARKER (ACTRESS FOUR)

Willard got me with child,
Knowing that I could not bring forth life
Without losing my own.
In my youth therefore I entered the portals of dust.
Traveler, it is believed in the village where I lived
That Henry loved me with a husband's love,
But I proclaim from the dust,
That he slew me to gratify his hatred.

WILLARD FLUKE (ACTOR THREE)

My wife lost her health,
And dwindled until she weighed scarce ninety pounds.
Then that woman, whom the men
Styled Cleopatra, came along
And we—we married ones
All broke our vows, myself among the rest.
Years passed and one by one
Death claimed them all in some hideous form,
And I was borne along by dreams
Of God's particular grace for me,
And I began to write, write, write, reams on reams
Of the second coming of Christ.
Then Christ came to me and said,
"Go into the church and stand before the congregation
And confess your sin."
But just as I stood up and began to speak, (*LIGHT goes
up on* ACTRESS TWO.)
I saw my little girl, who was sitting in the front seat—
My little girl who was born blind!
After that, all is blackness!

LOIS SPEARS (ACTRESS TWO)

Here lies the body of Lois Spears,

Born Lois Fluke, daughter of Willard Fluke,
Wife of Cyrus Spears,
Mother of Myrtle and Virgil Spears,
Children with clear eyes and sound limbs—
(I was born blind.)
I was the happiest of women
As wife, mother and housekeeper,
Caring for my loved ones,
And making my home
A place of order and bounteous hospitality:
For I went about the rooms,
And about the garden   (GIRL SINGER *hums*
With an instinct as sure as sight,   *first half of "I SEE*
As though there were eyes in my   *THE MOON."*)
  finger tips—
Glory to God in the highest.

GOD BLESS THE MOON—SONG (GIRL SINGER)
        . . . God bless the moon
        And God bless me

        And God bless the somebody
        I want to see.

SOW TOOK THE MEASLES—SONG (MALE SINGER)
How do you think I got on in the world?
I got me a sow and several other things.
The sow took the measles and she died in the spring.

What do you think that I made of her hide?
The very best saddle you ever did ride.
Saddles and bridles and other such things.
The sow took the measles and she died in the spring.

What do you think that I made of her nose?
The very best thimble that ever sewed clothes.
Thimbles and thread and other such things

Sow took the measles and she died in the spring.
What do you think I made of her feet?
The very best pickles you ever did eat.
Pickles and glue and other such things.
The sow took the measles and she died in the spring.

ABEL MELVENEY (ACTOR THREE)

I bought every kind of machine that's known—
Grinders, shellers, planters, mowers,
Mills and rakes and ploughs and threshers—
And all of them stood in the rain and sun,
Getting rusted, warped and battered,
For I had no sheds to store them in,
And no use for most of them.
And toward the last, when I thought it over,
There by my window, growing clearer
About myself, as my pulse slowed down,
And looked at one of the mills I bought—
Which I didn't have the slightest need of,
As things turned out, and I never ran—
A fine machine, once brightly varnished,
And eager to do its work,
Now with its paint washed off—
I saw myself as a good machine
That Life had never used.

HOD PUTT (ACTOR ONE)

Here I lie close to the grave
Of Old Bill Piersol,
Who grew rich trading with the Indians, and who
Afterwards took the bankrupt law
And emerged from it richer than ever.
Myself grown tired of toil and poverty
And beholding how Old Bill and others grew in wealth,
Robbed a traveler one night near Proctor's Grove,
Killing him unwittingly while doing so,
For the which I was tried and hanged.
That was my way of going into bankruptcy.

Now we who took the bankrupt law in our respective ways
Sleep peacefully side by side.

IDA FRICKEY (ACTRESS FOUR)

Nothing in life is alien to you:
I was a penniless girl from Summum
Who stepped from the morning train in Spoon River.
All the houses stood before me with closed doors
And drawn shades—I was barred out;
I had no place or part in any of them.
And I walked past the old McNeely mansion,
A castle of stone 'mid walks and gardens,
With workmen about the place on guard,
And the County and State upholding it
For its lordly owner, full of pride.
I was so hungry I had a vision:
I saw a giant pair of scissors
Dip from the sky, like the beam of a dredge,
And cut the house in two like a curtain.
But at the "Commercial" I saw a man,
Who winked at me as I asked for work—
It was Wash McNeely's son.
He proved the link in the chain of title
To half my ownership of the mansion,
Through a breach of promise suit—the scissors.
So, you see, the house, from the day I was born,
Was only waiting for me.

SILAS DEMENT (ACTOR ONE)

It was moonlight, and the earth sparkled
With new-fallen frost.
It was midnight and not a soul was abroad.
Out of the chimney of the court house
A greyhound of smoke leapt and chased
The northwest wind.
I carried a ladder to the landing of the stairs
And leaned it against the frame of the trap door
In the ceiling of the portico,

And I crawled under the roof and amid the rafters
And flung among the seasoned timbers
A lighted handful of oil-soaked waste.
Then I came down and slunk away.
In a little while the fire bell rang—
Clang! Clang! Clang!
And the Spoon River ladder company
Came with a dozen buckets and began to pour water
On the glorious bonfire, growing hotter,
Higher and higher, till the walls fell in,
And the limestone columns where Lincoln stood
Crashed like trees when the woodman fells them . . .
When I came back from Joliet prison
There was a new court house with a dome.
For I was punished like all who destroy
The past for the sake of the future.

(*Intro. by* MALE SINGER *on guitar,* "*THE WALKING BASE.*")

ANER CLUTE—DAILY FRASER
(ACTRESS TWO *plays on bench with* ACTRESS FOUR)
ANER CLUTE (ACTRESS TWO).
   Over and over they used to ask me,
   While buying the wine or the beer,
   In Peoria first, and later in Chicago,
   Denver, Frisco, New York, wherever I lived,
   How I happened to lead the life,
   And what was the start of it.
   Well, I told them a silk dress,
   And a promise of marriage from a rich man—
   It was Lucius Atherton.
   But that was not really it at all.
   Suppose a boy steals an apple
   From the tray at the grocery store,
   And they all begin to call him a thief,
   Wherever he goes, thief, thief, thief.
   The editor . . .

DAISY FRASER (ACTRESS FOUR).
  Did you ever hear of Editor Whedon
  Giving to the public treasury any of the
  Money he received for supporting
  Candidates for office?
ANER CLUTE (ACTRESS TWO).
  The minister . . .
DAISY FRASER (ACTRESS FOUR).
  Did you ever hear of Rev. Peet or Rev. Sibley
  Giving any part of their salary (earned by
  Keeping still, or speaking out as the leaders
  Wished them to do) to the
  Building of the waterworks?
ANER CLUTE (ACTRESS TWO).
  The judge . . .
DAISY FRASER (ACTRESS FOUR).
  Did you ever hear of the Circuit Judge
  Helping anyone except the "Q" Railroad
  And the bankers?
ANER CLUTE (ACTRESS TWO).
  The little boy can't get work, and he can't
  Get bread without stealing it. Why, the
  Little boy will steal. It is the way the
  People regard the theft of the apple, that
  Makes the little boy what he is.
DAISY FRASER (ACTRESS FOUR).
  But I . . . Daisy Fraser, who always passed
  Along the streets through rows of nods, and
  Smiles, and words such as, "There she goes,"
  Never was taken before Justice Arnett without con-
    tributing
  Ten dollars and cost to the school fund of
  Spoon River.

"INDIGNATION" JONES
(ACTRESS TWO *remains on bench with* ACTRESS FOUR
until introduced by ACTOR THREE.)

You would not believe, would you,
That I came from good Welsh stock?
That I was purer blooded than the
    white trash here?
And of more direct lineage than the
    New Englanders
And Virginians of Spoon River?
You would not believe that I had been
    to school
And read some books.
You saw me only as a run-down man,
With matted hair and beard
And ragged clothes.

(MALE SINGER
*underscores on
guitar with
"SPOON
RIVER"
music.*)

Sometimes a man's life turns into a cancer
From being bruised and continually bruised,
And swells into a purplish mass,
Like growths on stalks of corn.
Here was I, a carpenter, mired in a bog of life
Into which I walked, thinking it was a meadow,
With a slattern for a wife, and poor Minerva, my daugh-
    ter, (ACTRESS TWO *stands and comes to side of* ACTOR
        THREE.)
Whom you tormented and drove to death.
So I crept, crept, like a snail through the days
Of my life.
No more you hear my footsteps in the morning,
Resounding on the hollow sidewalk,
Going to the grocery store for a little corn meal
And a nickel's worth of bacon.

MINERVA JONES (ACTRESS TWO)

I am Minerva, the village poetess,
Hooted at, jeered at by the Yahoos of
    the street
For my heavy body, cock-eye, and
    rolling walk,
And all the more when "Butch" Weldy
Captured me after a brutal hunt.

(ACTRESS TWO
*moves to her
area.*)

He left me to my fate with Doctor Meyers; (ACTOR ONE
    rises.)
And I sank into death, growing numb from the feet up,
Like on stepping deeper and deeper into a stream of ice.
Will some one go to the village newspaper,
And gather into a book the verses I wrote?—
I thirsted so for love!
I hungered so for life!

DOCTOR MEYERS (ACTOR ONE)

No other man, unless it was Doc Hill,
Did more for people in this town than I.
And all the weak, the halt, the improvident
And those who could not pay flocked to me.
I was good-hearted, easy Doctor Meyers.
I was healthy, happy, in comfortable fortune,
Blest with a congenial mate, (ACTRESS FOUR *rises*.) my
    children raised,
All wedded, doing well in the world.
And then one night, Minerva, the poetess,
Came to me in her trouble, crying.
I tried to help her out—she died—
They indicted me, the newspapers disgraced me,
My wife perished of a broken heart.
And pneumonia finished me.

MRS. MEYERS (ACTRESS FOUR)

He protested all his life long
The newspapers lied about him villainously;
That he was not at fault for Minerva's fall,
But only tried to help her.
Poor soul so sunk in sin he could not see
That even trying to help her, as he called it,
He had broken the law human and divine.
Passers by, an ancient admonition to you;
If your ways would be ways of pleasantness,
And all your pathways peace,
Love God and keep His Commandments.

(The LIGHTS come up bright and full on the whole Stage.)

WHO KNOWS WHERE I'M GOIN'?—SONG
(MALE SINGER)
Who knows where I'm goin'?
Who knows what I'm after?
Happiness or sadness,
Love or hate or laughter.

(ACTRESS TWO *plays this with* ACTOR THREE *in his area. She vamps him, caresses him during the entire scene.*)

THE SIBLEYS (ACTRESS TWO & ACTOR THREE)
MRS. SIBLEY.
The secret of the soil—to receive seed.
The secret of the seed—the germ.
The secret of man—the sower.
The secret of woman . . .
REV. SIBLEY.
I loathed her.
As a termagant, as a wanton.
I knew of her adulteries, every one.
But even so, if I divorced the woman
I must forsake the ministry,
Therefore to do God's work and have it crop,
I bore with her!
So lied I to myself!
So lied I to Spoon River!
Yet I tried lecturing, ran for the legislature,
Canvassed for books,
With just one thought in mind:
If I make money thus, I will divorce her.

(ACTRESS TWO *returns to her bench.*)

MY ROOSTER—SONG (GIRL SINGER)
Oh, I love my little rooster
And my rooster loves me.
I'm going to cherish that rooster 'neath the green bay tree.
My little rooster goes

Cock a doodle doo doodle doo doodle doo.
Oh, I love my little guinea,
And my guinea loves me.
I'm going to cherish that guinea 'neath the green bay tree.
My little guinea goes patarack
But my rooster goes
Cock a doodle doo doodle doo doodle doo.
Oh, I love my little duckling
And my duckling loves me.
I'm going to cherish that duck 'neath the green bay tree.
My little duck goes quack quack,
My little guinea patarack,
But my rooster goes
Cock a doodle doo doodle doo doodle doo.

WILLIE METCALF (ACTOR ONE)

I was Willie Metcalf.
They used to call me "Doctor Meyers"
Because, they said, I looked like him.
And he was my father, according to Jack McGuire.
I lived in the livery stable,
Sleeping on the floor
Side by side with Roger Baughman's bulldog,
Or sometimes in a stall.
I could crawl between the legs of the wildest horses
Without getting kicked—we knew each other.
On spring days I tramped through the country
To get the feeling, which I sometimes
   lost,
That I was not a separate thing from the
   earth.
I used to lose myself, as if in sleep,
By lying with eyes half-open in the
   woods.
Sometimes I talked with animals—even
   toads and snakes—
Anything that had an eye to look into.
Once I saw a stone in the sunshine
Trying to turn into jelly.

(GIRL SINGER
*hums "I AM,
I AM."*)

In April days in this cemetery
The dead people gathered all about me,
And grew still, like a congregation in silent prayer.
I never knew whether I was a part of the earth
With flowers growing in me, or whether I walked—
Now I know.

I AM, I AM—SONG (GIRL SINGER)

I am the mountain,
I am the sky,
I am the swallow,
I fly and fly,
I am the meadow,
I nurse the lamb,
I am the river,
I am, I am.

We're bound together,
This world and me,
I am a part of
The things I see,
I am of nature,
It is of me,
I'm of my maker,
I am, I am.

A HORSE NAMED BILL—SONG (MALE SINGER)

I had a horse,
His name was Bill,
He ran so fast he couldn't stand still.
He ran away
One day
And I ran with him.
He ran so fast he couldn't stop,
He ran into a barber shop,
And fell exhausted
With his eye teeth
In the barber's left shoulder.

BATTERTON DOBYNS (ACTOR THREE)

Did my widow flit about
From Mackinac to Los Angeles,
Resting and bathing and sitting an hour
Or more at the table over soup and meats
And delicate sweets and coffee?
I was cut down in my prime
From overwork and anxiety.
But I thought all along, whatever happens
I've kept my insurance up,
And there's something in the bank,
And a section of land in Manitoba.
But just as I slipped I had a vision
In a last delirium:
I saw myself lying nailed in a box
With a white lawn tie and a boutonniere,
And my wife was sitting by a window
Some place afar overlooking the sea;
She seemed so rested, ruddy and fat,
Although her hair was white.
And she smiled and said to a colored waiter:
"Another slice of roast beef, George.
Here's a nickel for your trouble."

FLOSSIE CABANIS (ACTRESS FOUR)

From Bindle's Opera House in the village
To Broadway is a great step.
But I tried to take it, my ambition fired
When sixteen years of age,
Seeing "East Lynne" played here in the village
By Ralph Barrett, the coming
Romantic actor, who enthralled my soul.
True, I trailed back home, a broken failure,
When Ralph disappeared in New York,
Leaving me alone in the city—
But life broke him also.
In all this place of silence
There are no kindred spirits.
How I wish Duse could stand amid the pathos

Of these quiet fields
And read these words.

HORTENSE ROBBINS (ACTRESS TWO)

My name used to be in the papers daily
As having dined somewhere,
Or traveled somewhere,
Or rented a house in Paris,
Where I entertained the nobility.
I was forever eating or traveling,
Or taking the cure at Baden-Baden.
Now I am here to do honor
To Spoon River, here beside the family whence I sprang.
No one cares now where I dined,
Or lived, or whom I entertained,
Or how often I took the cure at Baden-Baden!

FRANK DRUMMER (ACTOR THREE)

Out of a cell into this darkened space—
The end at twenty-five!
My tongue could not speak what stirred within me,
And the village thought me a fool.
Yet at the start there was a clear vision,
A high and urgent purpose in my soul
Which drove me on trying to memorize
The Encyclopedia Britannica!

BARNEY HAINSFEATHER (ACTOR ONE)

If the excursion train to Peoria
Had just been wrecked, I might have escaped with my
    life—
Certainly I should have escaped this place.
But as it was burned as well, they mistook me
For John Allen who was sent to the Hebrew Cemetery
At Chicago,
And John for me, so I lie here.
It was bad enough to run a clothing store in this town,
But to be buried here—*ach!*

(*BLACKOUT. We now go back to area lighting.*)

SPOON RIVER—SONG (*Both singers*)
The meadow is flooded with white daffodils
The brook babbles on as it flows through the hills.
They haunt me, they hunt me wherever I roam.
Spoon River, Spoon River is callin' me home.

No matter how far I may wander away
Or what new land I find at the end of each day.
I'm haunted, I'm hunted wherever I roam
Spoon River, Spoon River is calling me home.

LUCINDA MATLOCK (ACTRESS FOUR)
I went to the dances at Chandlerville,
And played snap-out at Winchester.
One time we changed partners,
Driving home in the moonlight of middle
    June,
And then I found Davis.
We were married and lived together for
    seventy years,
Enjoying, working, raising the twelve
    children,
Eight of whom we lost
Ere I had reached the age of sixty.

(GIRL SINGER *humming obligato to "SPOON RIVER."*)

I spun, I wove, I kept the house, I nursed the sick,
I made the garden, and for holiday
Rambled over the fields where sang the larks,
And by Spoon River gathering many a shell,
And many a flower and medicinal weed—
Shouting to the wooded hills, singing to the green valleys.
At ninety-six I had lived enough, that is all,
And passed to a sweet repose.
What is this I hear of sorrow and weariness,
Anger, discontent and drooping hopes?
Degenerate sons and daughters,
Life is too strong for you—
It takes life to love life.

PETIT, THE POET (ACTOR THREE)

Seeds in a dry pod, tick, tick, tick,
Tick, tick, tick, like mites in a quarrel—
Faint iambics that the full breeze wakens—
But the pine tree makes a symphony thereof.
Triolets, villanelles, rondels, rondeaus,
Ballades by the score with the same old thought:
The snows and the roses of yesterday are vanished;
And what is love but a rose that fades?
Life all around me here in the village:
Tragedy, comedy, valor and truth,
Courage, constancy, heroism, failure—
All in the loom, and oh what patterns!
Woodlands, meadows, streams and rivers—
Blind to all of it all my life long.
Triolets, villanelles, rondels, rondeaus,
Seeds in a dry pod, tick, tick, tick,
Tick, tick, tick, what little iambics,
While Homer and Whitman roared in the pines?

ANNE RUTLEDGE (ACTRESS TWO)
(GIRL SINGER *hums "SPOON RIVER."*)

Out of me unworthy and unknown
The vibrations of deathless music:
"With malice toward none, with charity for all."
Out of me the forgiveness of millions toward millions,
And the beneficent face of a nation
Shining with justice and truth.
I am Anne Rutledge who sleep beneath these weeds,
Beloved in life of Abraham Lincoln,
Wedded to him, not through union,
But through separation.
Bloom forever, O Republic,
From the dust of my bosom!

SPOON RIVER—REPRISE (*Both singers*)
But once having left,
You can never return,
There is no going back,
There is only the yearn.

You're haunted, you're hunted,
Wherever you roam,
Spoon River, Spoon River
Is calling you home.

For the river is time
And it flows toward the sea,
And in leaving its banks,
You are free, you are free.

But you're haunted, you're hunted,
Wherever you roam,
Spoon River, Spoon River
Is calling you home.

(ACTOR ONE *crosses to Downstage Center*.)

ACTOR ONE

Good friends, let's to the fields*—I have a fever.
(**Other* ACTORS *rise and join him*. GIRL SINGER *continues
     humming till "I think I'll sleep."*)
After a little walk, and by your pardon,
I think I'll sleep. There is no sweeter thing,
Nor fate more blessed than to sleep. Here, world,
I pass you like an orange to a child.
I can no more with you. Do what you will . . .

END OF PLAY

Other Publications for Your Interest

GROWN UPS
(LITTLE THEATRE—COMEDY)

By JULES FEIFFER

2 men, 3 women, 1 female child—Interiors

An acerbic comedy by the famed cartoonist and author of *Knock Knock* and *Little Murders*. It's about a middle-aged journalist who has, at last, grown-up—only to find he's trapped in a world of emotional infants. "A laceratingly funny play about the strangest of human syndromes—the love that kills rather than comforts. Feiffer's vision seems merciless, but its mercy is the fierce comic clarity with which he exposes every conceivable permutation of smooth-tongued cruelty . . . Feiffer constructs a fiendishly complex machine of reciprocal irritation in which Jake (the journalist), his parents, his wife and his sister carp, cavil, harass, hector and finally attack one another with relentless trivia that detonate deeply buried resentments like emotional land mines . . . Moving past Broadway one-liners and easy gags, (Feiffer) makes laughter an adventure . . . This farce is Feiffer's exclusive specialty, and it's never been more harrowingly hilarious."—Newsweek. "Savagely funny."—N.Y. Times. "A compelling, devastating evening of theatre . . . the first adult play of the season."—Women's Wear Daily.   (#9125)

LUNCH HOUR
(LITTLE THEATRE—COMEDY)

By JEAN KERR

3 men, 2 women—Interior

Never has Jean Kerr's wit had a keener edge or her comic sense more peaks of merriment than in this clever confection, starring Gilda Radner and Sam Waterston as a pair whose spouses are having an affair, and who have to counter by inventing an affair of their own. He, ironically, is a marriage counsellor, and a bit of a stick. His wife juggles husband, lover and mother and is a real go-getter. In fact, it was she who proposed to him. Of the other couple, the wife is a bit kooky. She can discourse on things tacky while wearing an evening gown with her jogging sneakers on; or, again, be overjoyed at the prospect of a trip to Paris: "And we'll never have to ask for french fried potatoes. They'll just come like that." While her husband, "Well, he's rich for a living." Or as he expresses it: "It's very difficult to do something if you don't need any money." All ends forgivingly for both couples, as the aggrieved wife concedes that they both "need something to regret," and the other husband concedes "I knew when I married that everyone would want to dance with you." "Civilized, charming, stylish . . . Very warm and most amusing . . . delicately interweaves laughter and romance."—N.Y. Times. "An amiable comedy about the eternal quadrangle . . . The author's most entertaining play in years."—N.Y. Daily News. "A beautiful weave of plot, character and laughs . . . It's delicious."—NBC-TV.   (#674)

Other Publications for Your Interest

A WEEKEND NEAR MADISON
(LITTLE THEATRE—COMIC DRAMA)

By KATHLEEN TOLAN

2 men, 3 women—Interior

This recent hit from the famed Actors Theatre of Louisville, a terrific ensemble play about male-female relationships in the 80's, was praised by *Newsweek* as "warm, vital, glowing . . . full of wise ironies and unsentimental hopes". The story concerns a weekend reunion of old college friends now in their early thirties. The occasion is the visit of Vanessa, the queen bee of the group, who is now the leader of a lesbian/feminist rock band. Vanessa arrives at the home of an old friend who is now a psychiatrist hand in hand with her naif-like lover, who also plays in the band. Also on hand are the psychiatrist's wife, a novelist suffering from writer's block; and his brother, who was once Vanessa's lover and who still loves her. In the course of the weekend, Vanessa reveals that she and her lover desperately want to have a child—and she tries to persuade her former male lover to father it, not understanding that he might have some feelings about the whole thing. *Time Magazine* heard "the unmistakable cry of an infant hit . . . Playwright Tolan's work radiates promise and achievement." (#25051)

PASTORALE
(LITTLE THEATRE—COMEDY)

By DEBORAH EISENBERG

3 men, 4 women—Interior
(plus 1 or 2 bit parts and 3 optional extras)

"Deborah Eisenberg is one of the freshest and funniest voices in some seasons."—Newsweek. Somewhere out in the country Melanie has rented a house and in the living room she, her friend Rachel who came for a weekend but forgets to leave, and their school friend Steve (all in their mid-20s) spend nearly a year meandering through a mental landscape including such concerns as phobias, friendship, work, sex, slovenliness and epistemology. Other people happen by: Steve's young girlfriend Celia, the virtuous and annoying Edie, a man who Melanie has picked up in a bar, and a couple who appear during an intense conversation and observe the sofa is on fire. The lives of the three friends inevitably proceed and eventually draw them, the better prepared perhaps by their months on the sofa, in separate directions. "The most original, funniest new comic voice to be heard in New York theater since Beth Henley's 'Crimes of the Heart.'"—N.Y. Times. "A very funny, stylish comedy."—The New Yorker. "Wacky charm and wayward wit."—New York Magazine. "Delightful."—N.Y. Post. "Uproarious . . . the play is a world unto itself, and it spins."—N.Y. Sunday Times. (#18016)

NEW
BROADWAY COMEDIES
from
SAMUEL FRENCH, INC.

DIVISION STREET – DOGG'S HAMLET,
CAHOOT'S MACBETH – FOOLS – GOREY
STORIES – GROWNUPS – I OUGHT TO BE IN
PICTURES – IT HAD TO BE YOU – JOHNNY
ON A SPOT – THE KINGFISHER – A LIFE –
LOOSE ENDS – LUNCH HOUR – MURDER AT
THE HOWARD JOHNSON'S – NIGHT AND DAY –
ONCE A CATHOLIC – ROMANTIC COMEDY –
ROSE – SPECIAL OCCASIONS – THE SUICIDE
– THE SUPPORTING CAST – WALLY'S CAFE

For descriptions of plays, consult our   Basic Catalogue of Plays.